READ TOGETHER
WITH COZY & CUDDLE
BLOSSOM'S NEW HAT

Written by Elizabeth Taylor
Illustrated by Colin Petty

CLB

Colour Library Books

Blossom gave her old hat to Teeny Rabbit.

One sunny morning Blossom woke up feeling that today was going to be a special day. "I wonder why?" she asked herself. She looked around and saw her old, battered hat, with its faded paper flowers. "I know," she said. "It's because today I'm going to make myself a new, best hat." She was so happy, she gave her old hat to Teeny Rabbit to play with.

"My new hat," she said, "should have real flowers that smell nice. Paper flowers just smell like paper!" She put on a new straw hat. Then she set off to look for some flowers.

"Where are you going?" called Cuddle.

"To find some flowers for my new hat," said Blossom.

"Cozy Bear has lots of flowers," said Cuddle. "Let's go to see him."

Blossom put on a new straw hat.

Cozy put flowers on the hat.

"Hmm," said Cozy Bear, thoughtfully. "I know what kinds of flowers live in flower pots, but I'm not sure what kind are best for hats!"

"It's easy," said Blossom. "The kind that smell nice." She walked around the garden, sniffing every flower. Then she stopped. "These smell just right!" she cried.

Cozy put the flowers on Blossom's hat.

Blossom's new hat looked very pretty. Everywhere she went her hat was admired. "What a pretty hat," everybody said.

"Thank you," said Blossom. "It is, isn't it?"

That night, Blossom hung her new hat on the end of the bed so it would be the first thing she saw when she woke up.

Blossom's new hat looked very pretty.

But the flowers fell off in the night.

But in the morning, Blossom's new hat looked very sad. The pretty flowers had fallen off in the night! Blossom went to see Cuddle.

"My new hat is ruined. What shall I do?" she cried miserably.

"Cheer up, Blossom," said Cuddle. "We'll go to see Cozy Bear."

Cozy Bear knew what to do. "Soil!" said Cozy. "You need soil for the flowers to grow in, and flower pots to put the soil in . . ."

"But I want the flowers on my hat!" interrupted Blossom.

"Then we'll put the pots of flowers on the hat," said Cozy Bear, patiently. "That way they won't die."

Cozy Bear knew what to do.

Cuddle put some flowers into pots.

Cuddle and Cozy Bear set to work at once. Cuddle put some flowers into pots, and Cozy tied them to the hat. When it was finished, Blossom put the hat on and tottered over to the mirror.

Cozy tied the pots to Blossom's hat.

"It's lovely," she said, swaying from side to side.
"Isn't it a little heavy?" asked Cuddle, trying not to laugh.
"No, no, not at all," puffed Blossom. "Thank you so much!"

"Hello, bee," said Blossom as she walked home. "Do you like my hat?"

Buzz! went the bee. Then, suddenly, there were bees buzzing everywhere! The bees loved the hat!

"Oh no!" cried Blossom, and she ran all the way home.

The bees loved the hat. Blossom ran home.

Cuddle came to water the flowers.

Blossom sat in her favorite armchair for a little snooze. "My!" she said dreamily. "Fresh flowers do smell nice." Just then there was a knock at the door. It was Cuddle.

"I've come to water your flowers," he said, holding up a watering can. "Can I come in?"

Before Blossom could say "Of course," Cuddle climbed on to a stool and began to water the flowers on her hat. Blossom got very wet. Cold water ran down the back of her neck and over her ears. She began to wish she had her old hat back.

"Flowers need to be watered regularly," declared Cuddle.

Blossom wished she had her old hat back.

But Blossom had had enough of bees and watering cans and hats that were too heavy. She went straight around to Mrs. Rabbit's house.

"Here's your hat," said Teeny. She was playing with it in the wash-tub! It was all wet and soggy.

"Oh no!" said Blossom, faintly. "It's ruined."

Teeny was playing with the old hat in the bath. It was all wet.

Mrs. Rabbit hung it on the washing line.

Now, Mrs. Rabbit was very good at listening, so she listened to Blossom, who told her all about her new hat.

"Never mind," she said calmly, "I'll hang your old hat on the washing line to dry and it will be as good as new in no time."

Everyone waited patiently. The wind blew and the sun shone and soon the hat was dry.

"Look!" said Cuddle. "The paper flowers are as bright as they ever were."

"So they are," said Blossom, happily. She tried on the hat and gave a little sniff. "What a smell!" she cried.

Everyone waited for the hat to dry.

"Oh dear," said Mrs. Rabbit. "I'm sorry! It must be the soap from the wash-tub. I'll wash it again to get rid of the smell."

"No, no!" cried Blossom. "It smells just like fresh flowers. It's just what I wanted." Blossom's old hat really was as good as new.

"And it will be a lot less trouble!" laughed Cuddle.

Soon the old hat was as good as new.